Once upon a time, a boy named Bruno wished for his very own guinea pig.

Not so far away, in a little glass box, a tiny guinea pig named Titch

waited for his Big Person to come and find him. . . .

For my dad

TO DO:

1. Get my guinea pig

2. Play lots of games

First U.S. edition 2014

Library of Congress Catalog Card Number 2013953101

ISBN 978-0-7636-7316-1

14 15 16 17 18 19 WKT 10 9 8 7 6 5 4 3 2 1

Printed in Shenzhen, Guangdong, China

This book was typeset in PMN Caecilia.
The illustrations were done in pen and watercolor.

Candlewick Press
99 Dover Street
Somerville, Massachusetts 02144

visit us at www.candlewick.com

some are spotty

BRUNO and TITCH

The Tale of a Boy and His Guinea Pig

SHEENA DEMPSEY

CANDLEWICK PRESS

I've been waiting three human weeks for
a Big Person to come and bring me home.
In guinea-pig time, that's almost a year.
Which is a VERY long time to wait.

No matter how hard I try
(and I try R-E-A-L-L-Y hard) . . .

the Big People always choose some other guinea pig instead.

Here's another Big Person right now.

I bet he's not here for me, though. They never are.

Wait! Maybe . . . maybe he IS here for me!

It's finally happening!

My very own Big Person AT LAST!

MRS. PINKERLEY'S PETS
OUTBREAK!!
FLEA
EPIDEMIC!
Ouch! Not so tight, Bruno!
LOST!
OPEN
Puppy Training! ASK INSIDE
19.99
Come say hello to the Kittens.
WELCOME

LOOK!

A house! A real, live Big Person house.

I can't believe it. I've made it.

"Welcome to your new home, Titch!" says Bruno.

My new home is . . . different.

Bruno eats strange food. He gets up very early.

And we don't always like the same things.

More than anything,
Bruno likes to play. A LOT.
And I love to play as much
as the next guinea pig,
but there's only
so much
of the

Bouncing-
Very-High
Game

This is not fun for me.

I can take.

Or the
Very-Scary-
Balloon
Game

I like to stay on the ground,
where my favorite
game is hiding.
It's quiet.
Not too high
or bouncy
or fast.

Beware!
Dangerous
Aminals!

When we're not playing, Bruno and I
look at stuff together.

And we make all
kinds of important things.

Guinea Pig Air

← Like this.
It's an airy plane.

PHYSICS
of
FLIGHT

So even though we're different,
I think Bruno and I are
becoming the best of friends.

At least that's what I thought.

This morning, Bruno started
acting all strange.

He looked at me with
his BIG eye.

He drew some pictures
that I didn't understand.

poo goes in here

poo hut

guinea pig door

What does all this mean?

Guinea Pigs Like Froot

and Vegtobbels

Guinea Pigs sometimes need to rest

What's he *doing*
in there?

Maybe Bruno is bored of me already.

Is he going to get rid of me?

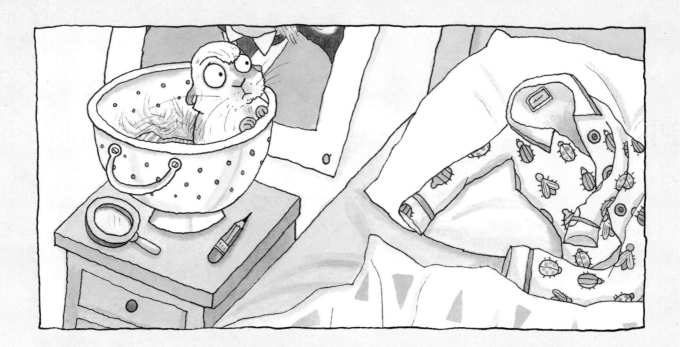

Where did he go?

Why hasn't he taken me
out of my bed yet?
This is not a good sign.

Maybe
he doesn't want
to be friends anymore?

Here he comes.

Please
don't send
me back to the
glass box!

LOOK! A guinea-pig palace!

In all my guinea-pig life (3 months and 3 weeks),
I've never seen anything so incredible!
"Behold my great guinea-pig
palace of fun, Titch!
I hope you like it,"
says Bruno.

Only a true best friend could know all of my favorite things.

My own jacuzzi.

A fruit-salad bar.

(So delicious.)

Some privacy.

Poo HuT (private)

(I really need that.)

And a proper bed with
my favorite food nearby.

I waited a long time for my Big Person.

But now I have Bruno. And he has me.